Bitter Chocolate

Sally Grindley

BLOOMSBURY

LONDON BERLIN NEW YORK SYDNEY

Bloomsbury Publishing, London, Berlin, New York and Sydney

First published in Great Britain in June 2010 by Bloomsbury Publishing Plc
50 Bedford Square, London, WC1B 3DP

A CIP catalogue record for this book is available from the British Library

ISBN 978 0 7475 9502 1

MIX
Paper from
responsible sources
FSC® C018072

Typeset by Hewer Text UK Ltd, Edinburgh
Printed in Great Britain by Clays Ltd, St Ives plc, Bungay, Suffolk

5 7 9 10 8 6 4

www.bloomsbury.com/childrens
www.sallygrindley.co.uk

For Bloomsbury Qatar Foundation Publishing

Chapter 1

'Did you ever kill anyone?'

The question flew like a bullet through the tense dark of the night and hit Pascal hard in the chest. He had thought Kojo was asleep. Hadn't he heard and been surprised by the stillness of his friend not so very long ago? Now the silence was shot into tiny fragments by the blast of those five words.

'Did you? Did you ever kill anyone?'

'What's it to you?'

'Just wondered. Just wondered what it feels like.'

'Maybe I don't want to talk about it.' Pascal turned over on to his other side, so that he was facing away from Kojo. The wooden pallet was hard underneath his shoulder. He put his hand over the place where the jagged, lumpy scar from an old knife wound rubbed uncomfortably against the planks.

1

'You talk in your sleep sometimes,' Kojo persisted.

'You fart in your sleep,' Pascal countered. 'Like a machine gun – *phut-phut-phut*.'

He waited for the retort, but it didn't come. Instead, he heard his friend scramble to his feet and pad over to the barred window. He was used to Kojo's restlessness. He was used to the nightly conversations, though he hadn't been prepared for tonight's question. He should have been prepared. It was such an obvious question to ask someone if you weren't emotionally involved with the answer.

Neither of the boys ever slept well, regardless of how hard they worked during the day, regardless of the long hours they spent toiling under the baking sun. *None* of them slept well, for there were ten other boys sharing the decrepit outhouse that passed as their home. It was hot and filthy and airless. Besides, there were too many ghosts lurking in the dead of the night, ready to ambush them the minute they were off their guard.

'Sometimes I think I'll see my mother again soon,' said Kojo quietly. 'Sometimes I think I'll be walking along a path and she'll appear in front of me. Or she'll turn up at the plantation and tell me it's time I came home because my food's getting cold. Do you ever think that?'

Pascal didn't answer. There was no need. His friend wasn't expecting an answer this time, especially if it was an answer urging him to abandon his fool's dreams.

'I don't know what I'd do if I did see her. I probably wouldn't believe it was her at first, and then I'd want to throw myself into her arms. But I'd probably pass out from the shock instead.'

'You're such a girl, you probably would pass out,' Pascal mocked. 'Then your poor mother would weep over you, thinking you had died of fright.'

'If I could just find out that she's all right,' said Kojo. 'And my brother and Papa. I keep thinking that Papa might have a new job and that it would be fine for me to go home. But he wasn't well enough.'

Silence filled the room again.

Pascal closed his eyes and tried to picture his own mother's face – not the face she had worn the last time he saw her alive, but the one that belonged to happier days. It eluded him, as it so often did, languishing in the murky shadows beyond his grasp. Next, he scoured his memory for his father and his elder sister, Angeline. They drifted towards him, fading in and out of focus. At the point when he could almost make out the details of their faces, they were blown away by a sudden flash of bright light and a deafening explosion.

Seconds later, Angeline reappeared, beckoned at him to follow her, then disappeared once more.

'If I made a ton of money, I'd send it all to my family so that they could buy things again and then I'd be able to go home. That's what I'd do, and nobody would be able to stop me,' Kojo said.

'How are you going to make a ton of money when most of the time they don't bother to pay us?'

'I'm not staying here for ever. One day I'm going to be a doctor, then they'll pay me proper money.'

'Oh yeah, and one day I'm going to build me a plane and fly me back home. How are you going to be a doctor when you don't even go to school?'

'I'm going back to school. One day. When I run away from here.'

'They'll beat you if you try to run away.'

'They won't catch me. I'll be too quick for them.'

'Huh! A snail could run faster than you.'

'Why do you always have to stamp all over my dreams?'

Pascal felt a stab of guilt. Why couldn't he just let his friend believe what he wanted to believe? What did he have to gain by bringing him down to earth every time?

'Because dreams make what's real seem even worse, that's why,' he said at last.

'You can't live without dreams,' said Kojo.

'Yes, I can,' Pascal sighed.

'I don't believe you.'

'Believe what you like.'

'I bet you hope just as much as I do.'

'I'll tell you what I hope. I hope you'll shut up for five minutes so that I can get some sleep,' Pascal snapped.

'I don't see why *you* should sleep when you keep me awake with your talking,' Kojo said sulkily.

Pascal growled through his teeth. His irritation threatened to unleash itself on his friend. 'If I talk in my sleep I can't help it,' he hissed. 'You talk when you're awake and I'm trying to sleep – yack, yack, yack, blah, blah, blah – and you can help it, but you don't because you're a selfish heap of dung. Now shut up, or else.'

There was a long silence between them, broken only by the shuffling of Kojo's feet as he found his way back to bed.

And then, just as Pascal closed his eyes and allowed himself to relax, he heard Kojo mutter, 'You wait. If I do find a way to get out of here, I'm not going to take you with me. No way.'

Chapter 2

Pascal sat in the front seat of an abandoned car on the outskirts of his village.

'Where are we going, then, driver?' asked Olivier.

Pascal thought for a moment. 'Kissidougou,' he said.

'Yeah, Kissidougou,' yelled Bobo from the back seat.

'Nah, I want to go to Conakry,' Kamil argued, leaning forward over Pascal's shoulder.

'No way,' said Pascal. 'It's too far.'

'You gonna pay for the petrol, Kamil?' sniggered Olivier.

'Let's go, let's go,' said Bobo.

'Kissidougou's boring,' grumbled Kamil.

Pascal pretended to turn a key in the ignition. As one, all four boys started to make engine noises and bounce up and down in their seats. When Pascal leant to the right, the others leant to the right. When he leant to the left, the others followed suit.

'Hold on,' he said. 'Pothole coming up.'

They held on to the rusty doorframes, and when Pascal counted 'One, two, three', they leapt in the air and landed with a universal 'Aw, that was a big one!'

'My turn to drive now,' said Kamil.

'But we've only just set off,' protested Pascal. 'I've only been driver for two seconds.'

'You're driving like a tortoise,' said Kamil. 'You're in the back now.' He had already left his seat and was standing by Pascal's side, pulling at Pascal's T-shirt to make him move.

Pascal didn't want to move. He wanted to be the one to decide if there were potholes in the road, or cows to be avoided, or hens to be driven at.

'Move, will you?' insisted Kamil.

Pascal looked at him sullenly, but slid off the seat and let him take the wheel. He stood by the side of the car.

'Hold on tight, everyone,' Kamil yelled. 'We're off to Conakry and we're not hanging about.'

'Jump in, Pascal. You don't want to walk, do you?' laughed Olivier.

'I think he's sulking,' piped up Bobo.

'I'm not sulking,' retorted Pascal.

'We're on our way,' cried Kamil. 'I've got the accelerator all the way to the bottom.'

The three boys began making engine noises again, twice as loudly as before, and bumped up and down so hard that the car shook and rattled on its wheel-less axles.

'Bye-bye, Pascal.' Olivier grinned and waved.

'Don't blame me if you run out of petrol,' Pascal said, sniffing loudly as he sloped away.

He was hoping his cousins would beg him to come back, to hear them say that he could be the driver again. They didn't, though. They carried on as if it didn't matter that he was no longer there with them.

'Who cares?' Pascal said out loud, kicking at a stone that lay on the path in front of him and losing his sandal in the process.

All of a sudden, the day had stopped being fun. It had begun with school, and Pascal liked school, as long as he didn't have to stand up in front of everybody and answer questions. He liked to sit at the back, by the window, where it wasn't such a crush, and where he could look out across the fields whenever lessons dragged on. Mostly, that was when the subject was English. He struggled so hard with English, and he didn't see the point of it. Surely one language was enough to get by with, and he was never likely to meet an Englishman. Or an American. Or an Australian. And if he did, he wouldn't talk to them. It was bad enough in class, when his teacher asked him to say a word in English out loud. The sniggers always sounded worse when he said something than when anyone else had a go. Yet his parents kept telling him how important it was for him to master such an important subject and that it would help him to get a good job. They couldn't speak English themselves, apart from 'hello' and 'please', but they told him that the world was changing fast and that a good command of English was one of the secrets of success.

There hadn't been an English lesson that day. Pascal had been able to enjoy two of his favourite lessons, maths and science, as well as helping in the school garden and learning manual skills. If anyone ever asked what he dreamt of being when he was older, his reply was that he wanted to use his hands, perhaps as a builder, or even an engineer, though he didn't really understand what engineers did. He knew that he wasn't going to be an office worker or a teacher, and he hated the thought of working at the diamond mines like his father, even though his father was a manager and Pascal was proud of him.

After school, Pascal and his cousins, with a number of their friends, had played football on the makeshift pitch behind the school building. He wasn't particularly good at football, but his father had bought him a Barcelona shirt two years earlier and Pascal still wore it, even though it was too small. He was wearing it that day, hoping as usual that some of Rivaldo's brilliance would rub off on him, so that everyone would want him on their side, rather than pushing him out on to the wing and then ignoring him. For once it worked. The ball accidentally found him, stuck to his feet as he dribbled over the rutted ground, and flew from his foot right between the two wooden sticks that marked out the goal.

'How did you do that?' Kamil had exclaimed.

'Great goal!' Bobo cheered.

'Hey, littl'un, where did that come from?' Olivier cried.

Pascal couldn't explain it and wished he could relive every minute of the goal in slow motion. He remembered the feeling of triumph, though, as he made his way down the village street, past Mr Bon in his bicycle repair shop, past the bush taxi, past his aunt, who was braiding Olivier's sister's hair, past the empty marketplace, and on until the shops gave way to groups of scattered houses with hens scratching around outside and lines of washing laced in between. At this point, the street was little more than a dusty track, which branched right and left, linking the houses together.

When he rounded the bamboo fence that separated their homestead from the pathway, Pascal could see his mother standing near the front door of their home, his baby sister, Bijou, balanced on her hip. In the courtyard to the side, his elder sister, Angeline, was pounding rice in a mortar.

'Pascal, my child, how has your day been?' his mother called.

'I scored a great goal when we played football,' Pascal replied. 'You should have seen it, Maman! I ran and ran, and no one could catch me and I kicked it hard, straight between the posts.'

'And there was me thinking you didn't like football,' his mother said, smiling. 'Did you have a good day at school? And how are you getting on with your lessons?'

'I had a good day, Maman,' said Pascal. He took Bijou from her and let his baby sister pull at his hair. 'Ow, ow, ow!' he squealed, before tickling her ribs and laughing at her giggles.

'It's nice to see you looking so happy, little brother,' Angeline called over.

'I wish Papa had been there to see me score my goal,' Pascal replied. 'I wish he didn't have to go away to work all the time.'

Chapter 3

Pascal knew a little about the fighting that was going on in Sierra Leone and Liberia. He'd heard his parents and some of the other villagers talking about it, and occasionally it was mentioned on the radio. He knew that refugees from those countries were pouring over the border into his own country, Guinea, and that camps were being set up to house them not so far from where his family lived. He'd wondered vaguely what it would be like to live in a country at war, and whether he would want to stay there or run away to a foreign place, where he wouldn't know anyone and where they might not even speak the same language or eat the same food. He thought he would probably want to stay put, and that it might even be quite exciting, as long as the fighting wasn't too close by. But this conflict seemed very remote from his own life in a village, where everybody was friends with, or related to, everybody else.

Sometimes Pascal heard his parents complaining that the huge number of refugees was costing their country too much money.

'We can barely afford to feed our own people,' his father said, 'let alone all these others.'

'But they can't go back, can they, Papa?' Pascal said. 'They might be killed if they go back.'

'No, I suppose they can't. We can only hope that the fighting stops, and soon. Then there won't be any excuses.'

'It can't be much fun living in a refugee camp,' Angeline responded. 'Surely they're not going to be making excuses not to go home.'

'Unless the fighting goes on for so long that they have nothing to go home to,' their father observed.

Pascal was glad that his own country was peaceful, though he joined in with his cousins and friends at playing shoot-'em-up games. Sometimes they rampaged through the surrounding forest, whooping and hollering at the top of their voices, threatening violence against each other and acting dead or wounded. Pascal wasn't sure how much he enjoyed the sheer riotousness of it all, and so he would hang around on the fringes, hoping not to be noticed, but taking part just enough that no one, particularly Kamil, could accuse him of 'cowardice'. At times it made him feel vulnerable, like if he found himself alone and hid by a tree, heart pounding, certain that someone would be creeping up on him, but not knowing from which direction. The forest played its own tricks too. Branches would suddenly lurch or creak, bushes would shiver, small animals would dart out from the undergrowth by his feet, and monkeys would hurl sticks from their treetop playground.

By the time a game had run its course and the boys had headed home, still loud and boisterous, Pascal couldn't wait to immerse himself in the relative quiet of his family and chores. He would happily feed the chickens and collect their eggs, or bounce baby Bijou on his lap, while his mother and Angeline prepared their evening meal.

'You boys,' Mrs Camara would say, smiling. 'We could hear the racket you were making all over the village. I expect they could hear it in the Côte d'Ivoire.'

'I'm surprised the monkeys haven't packed their bags and moved out,' Angeline said more than once.

'It's fun,' Pascal insisted. He really could mean it when he wasn't in the middle of a fight, and objected if his mother ever tried to suggest that he was a sensitive child, a bit of a loner and perhaps not cut out for the rough and tumble of boyhood, especially when his father once added that he needed to toughen up, to be more like his cousins.

'Why does he have to be like his cousins?' his mother argued. 'That Kamil could do with a little of Pascal's gentleness.'

'I'm just saying that he won't get anywhere in life if he doesn't stand up for himself,' his father replied.

'I do stand up for myself when I have to, Papa,' Pascal protested. 'I'm just not loud and bossy like Kamil.'

'Kamil will go far,' said Mr Camara.

'Why do you think that, Papa? He's always missing school and when he's there he messes about. And his English is far worse than mine.'

'He's a leader. People will follow him.'

'Not if he's ignorant. Certainly not for long,' Pascal's mother replied. 'Anyway, he's two years older than Pascal. Why do you expect our son to have such confidence at the age of ten? I tell you, he'll be fine if

you leave him be. Children are all different, and Pascal
will deal with things in his own way.'

Pascal's father shrugged his shoulders and muttered,
'I guess you're right', while his mother hurried
outside, loudly clattering the pans she was carrying.
He grinned at Pascal. 'You'll find that with women,'
he said. 'They're always right. At least, you have to let
them think they are.'

'Maman *is* right,' said Pascal. 'And I know how to
look after myself.'

Chapter 4

Every so often, the noise of gunfire could be heard in the village now. Pascal didn't know what it was initially. The distant *rat-a-tat-a-tat* sounded as if it might be loggers or a carpenter or a stonemason at work, but when it happened in the middle of the night, Pascal began to ask questions.

Mrs Camara shrugged her shoulders when, in the absence of his father, he asked her for the first time.

'There are all sorts of strange noises in the night,' she said. 'I don't know which ones you mean.'

'It's not just in the night,' said Pascal. 'Sometimes you can hear them in the daytime too.'

His mother shrugged once more. 'I'm sure it's nothing to worry about.' She smiled and carried on with her washing, humming quietly.

Pascal was sure she was hiding something, and asked

his cousins what they thought the noise was. They laughed loudly at him.

'That's gunfire you're hearing, dolt,' Kamil sniggered. He placed a pretend gun at Pascal's head. 'Bang, bang, you're dead!'

Pascal pushed his hand away. He thought Kamil meant that someone was practising shooting, until Olivier added, 'There are rebel soldiers all around us, waiting to grab us when we're asleep.'

The cousins laughed again. Pascal tried to laugh with them, even though he couldn't see the joke.

'Poor Pascal, he won't sleep a wink ever again,' Kamil snorted.

'Yes, I will, because I don't believe you,' Pascal retorted lamely.

'Believe what you like,' said Olivier.

Pascal wanted to believe that it was all just stupid talk, but when he spoke to Angeline, she failed to douse his suspicion that something bad was happening.

'Why can't you tell me what's going on?' he asked. 'I'm not a baby.'

'It's nothing to be concerned about,' she replied. 'It's a few rogue soldiers from across the border firing a few shots to make themselves feel big.'

'But how far away are they?' Pascal wanted to know.

'Far enough,' said Angeline. 'And our soldiers will soon send them packing.'

Try as they might to prevent him from worrying, his family couldn't stop him from listening to the gossip at school. Some of the children had heard that rebels had taken control of a number of nearby towns and that there was fierce fighting. Others said that the refugees from Sierra Leone and Liberia were causing trouble because they wanted to go home.

Pascal wished his father would come home and stay home. He was scared that he might be caught up in the fighting while he was away, and that they might never see him again. Besides, he wanted his father to be there to protect them.

'What if Papa is at work and the rebels come here?' he said to Angeline. 'What will we do?'

'They won't come here. There's no reason for them to come here.' Angeline tried to reassure him, but Pascal could tell that she was anxious herself.

'What are they fighting about, anyway?'

'I don't really know. Perhaps they just want change. Perhaps they want a better life and fighting is the only way they can think of to get it.'

*

One morning, a crackled news bulletin on the radio in the village shop told of people being attacked in another village.

'Is that village near here?' Pascal asked his mother as she hurriedly paid for her groceries and shunted him outside.

Mrs Camara shook her head and busied herself with Bijou.

Olivier saw them from across the road and dashed over to them, greeting his aunt politely. To Pascal he said, 'Did you hear the explosions last night? They sounded really close.'

'Sound travels,' Mrs Camara broke in. 'You'll find they were many kilometres away.'

'Papa doesn't think so,' replied Olivier. 'He sleeps by the door at night with an axe and a knife.'

'Your father has always been over-cautious.'

Olivier looked somewhat taken aback by this criticism of his father by his aunt.

Mrs Camara sensed his unease and patted him on the arm. 'It never does any harm, though,' she said.

Together they walked back to their homesteads and no further mention was made of explosions or fighting.

As they approached, Pascal was delighted to see his father. He was carrying a large piece of wood across their yard, but put it down as soon as he saw them. Pascal ran to him, cheering loudly.

'Hey, Papa,' he called. 'I thought you weren't coming home till the end of the month.'

'Well, I decided to come home early and spend some time with my family.' He smiled, squeezing Pascal's shoulder.

He gave his wife a hug, then lifted Bijou high above his head. She wriggled and squealed with pleasure. They went indoors, where Angeline was preparing their meal.

The conversation over dinner that evening revolved mostly around Mr Camara's work at the diamond mines. Mrs Camara regularly steered the talk back to this topic if it looked like it was heading towards more sombre subjects. There were things Pascal wanted to ask his father, but he soon realised that his mother wouldn't allow their time together to be spoiled, and in any case he was happy just to have his father there. Pascal didn't want to follow in his footsteps, but he loved hearing about how he passed his days and the people he worked with. As a manager, his father didn't have to pan for diamonds himself, but that didn't stop Pascal wanting to know everything about the process of searching for diamonds and what happened when a worker found one.

'What's the biggest diamond anyone's ever found?' he asked. 'Can the person who found the diamond keep it? How much do you get paid if you find a diamond?'

Pascal especially liked listening to stories about what the miners did when they were off duty. Mr Camara and his fellow managers seemed to spend many hours playing card games, or watching sport on television in a bar in the nearby town, or kicking a ball around with the local townspeople.

'I wish we had a television,' Pascal said when he heard that they had watched the national team playing football against rival Malawi.

'We only drew,' said Mr Camara. 'We threw away a one-goal lead, so you didn't miss anything.'

Pascal asked him, not for the first time, if he would teach him some card games. Not for the first time, his father promised that he would one day soon. Pascal wished he meant it, but he always seemed to have more important things to do when he came home. Sometimes Pascal felt that he would never be important in his father's life and that he disappointed him because he was too quiet.

Before he went to bed that night, he asked his father how long he was staying.

'Just as long as it takes,' Mr Camara replied.

'As long as what takes?'

'I have a few things to do and then I must go back – unless you're planning to provide for us instead of me.'

Nevertheless, Pascal went to bed that night happy in the knowledge that both of his parents were there to protect him if anything bad happened. And he made up his mind that he would ask his father what he thought about the rebels and the fighting, whether or not his mother wanted it discussed. He lay listening to the sounds of the night – cicadas, tree frogs, monkeys, cattle, the low voices of his parents talking – and wondered if he would hear gunfire that night. Would it wake his father and, if so, what would his father do?

Chapter 5

The plantation bell. Not ringing, but clanging, harsh and discordant. Six o'clock in the morning. Still dark. Muffled groans, mumbled complaints. The bell, continuous, demanding. Ghostly shapes clawing their way out through the deep cushions of sleep and struggling to their feet.

Pascal rolled on to his back. How much sleep had he had? It felt as if he had only just closed his eyes, only just listened to Kojo's mutterings.

A cigarette would be good right now, he thought.

He made an 'o' with his mouth and practised exhaling. It had been over a year since he had last smoked, but he hadn't quite lost the addiction he had developed as a soldier. The first time a cigarette had been thrust at him, already lit, he had nearly choked on it. He had tried to refuse the second one, only to be warned that if he didn't obey orders he would be thrashed. He didn't know at what point his body had made the transition from loathing every minute of every drag to craving the next one. It wasn't a craving now, not any more, just a nagging mechanical memory of the habit.

The scuffling increased around him. The voices crescendoed, distorted at first through crusty mouths, then shrill and incessant. They managed to sound full of excitement at the unfolding of a new day, even though there was nothing to be excited about, except perhaps the knowledge that they were going to be fed in a few minutes' time.

'You gonna stay there all day?' Kojo was standing above him in the gloom.

'What's it to you if I do?' asked Pascal.

'Nothing.' Kojo shrugged. 'You'll get into trouble if you don't hurry up, that's all.'

'*You'll get into trouble if you don't hurry up,*' Pascal mimicked. 'I'm so scared I think I might wet my pants.'

'Sometimes you're not much of a friend,' said Kojo.

'You're not going to take me with you if you escape,' Pascal jibed. 'That's not very friendly.'

He could see Kojo hovering, unsure of what to do next. They usually headed off for breakfast together, but Kojo didn't know whether to go now with the others and leave Pascal behind, or to wait for Pascal and risk being late himself.

'You two coming, then?' Tiene, one of the other boys, asked.

'I'll catch you up,' Pascal sighed.

He was so bored with the endless routine of it all. He was so desperate for some space just to be. What could they do to him, anyway? He'd had plenty of beatings before. It would be worth a beating to spend just five minutes alone, five minutes lying there in the darkness and quiet, freed from the constant maelstrom of activity that living with so many other boys inflicted upon him. Free to pursue his own thoughts wherever they took him, as long as it wasn't to the carefully delineated no-go areas of his mind.

How long would it be before his absence was noticed and somebody was dispatched to find him? It wouldn't be many minutes, Pascal knew that much, and he didn't want to waste his time worrying about it. There were things that he needed to pull back into focus, things that he couldn't seem to grasp during the monotonous yet exhausting passage of each day. The one certainty was that he had to get back to his own country and find out if his mother and his sisters were still alive. If he discovered that they were, it would make everything he had gone through easier to reconcile.

Pascal lurched to his feet and stood at the window. It was nearly light outside now that the sun was breaking through. It was going to be hot again, insufferably hot, but they would all be expected to carry on with their work regardless. On days like these, some of the younger boys came close to passing out, yet the overseers showed them no mercy, shouting: 'This ain't no holiday camp. You ain't paid good money to slack. Put some effort in or there ain't gonna be no food for you tonight.'

Pascal had tried to intervene once when one of the eight-year-olds collapsed from sickness and hunger. He had lifted him up and carried him to his bed. For that, he'd received a lashing round his legs with a bicycle chain, a warning to mind his own business and a fine for absenting himself from work without permission.

He could hear the sound of tin plates clanking and the boys' voices, loud and garrulous. He moved away from the window. He hadn't chosen to be alone to spend the time listening to them. He looked round the dilapidated wooden shack that had served as his home for the last eleven months. He had just turned thirteen when he arrived, and was now one of the oldest boys working on the plantation. The thought of it depressed him. What would happen when the overseers decided that he had served his purpose? He might be desperate to leave, but he wanted it to be on his terms and when he was ready, not when they felt like throwing him out. He had had enough of other people determining the when and where of his life. He had had enough of being bullied and pushed around, shouted at and intimidated. At least when he had been drugged . . . but that was a no-go area.

Pascal heard footsteps approaching and knew that his time was up. He might just as well have gone to breakfast with the others for all he had achieved by staying behind. He kicked at one of the wooden pallets that the boys slept on, then walked out of the shack.

'What d'you think you're doin' loiterin' around 'ere when you're supposed to be at breakfast?' It was Le Cochon, the worst of the overseers and the one who had hit him with the bicycle chain. His real name was Mr Kouassi, but the boys had nicknamed him 'Le Cochon' because he was fat and because of the way he ate his food.

'I wasn't hungry,' said Pascal.

'Not 'ungry, eh? We must be feedin' you too well. Is that right?'

Pascal stared at him defiantly. 'Corn paste doesn't do it for me any more,' he muttered.

'Gettin' fussy, are we?' Le Cochon sneered. 'I reckon we should be grateful, don't you?'

Pascal stared at the ground.

'Don't you?' Le Cochon said threateningly.

Pascal nodded briefly. A heavy stick caught him on the elbow. He winced with pain.

'Get to work before I find the other arm, and since we've been feedin' you too well, there ain't gonna be no food for you tonight.' Mr Kouassi marched away.

Pascal rubbed his elbow. 'If I had my way, I'd wipe your stupid corn paste all over your stupid fat face,' he growled under his breath. He headed off towards the field, rueing the fact that he would only be eating a measly lunch that day.

Kojo came over to him as he collected a machete from the store. 'I got you a banana,' he whispered. 'It's in my pocket. You can have it when no one's looking.'

'You're an idiot!' Pascal hissed. 'They'll take the skin off your back if they find out you've been nicking food.'

'They won't find out, unless you tell them. I thought you'd be hungry.'

'Look, I don't want you taking risks for me, OK?' Pascal looked at Kojo's scowling face. 'But thanks,' he added. 'Come on, let's go and beat the hell out of those pods.'

Chapter 6

Pascal was woken the next morning by the sound of his parents talking loudly. They were outside, but their voices carried through the open door. He wondered if they were arguing, and tried to still his breathing so that he could hear what they were saying. It went quiet for a while, then Bijou began to cry and their mother hurried indoors to pick her up.

'Where's Papa?' Pascal called.

'He's gone into the village,' Mrs Camara replied.

'He's not going back to work today, is he?' Pascal called, jumping to his feet and clambering into his shorts.

'No, not today,' Mrs Camara said.

'Tomorrow, then?'

'Why are you so keen for him to go?'

'I'm not,' Pascal protested. 'I don't want him to

go at all. I want him to stay and teach me some card games and play football with me. He keeps saying he will.'

'Your father has a lot of jobs to do while he's here.'

'What sort of jobs? Can I help him?'

'Well, the fence needs repairing,' Mrs Camara said carefully. 'You might be able to help him with that.'

'That's not difficult. I can help with that,' Pascal said eagerly.

'We'll see what he says when he comes back.'

Pascal wished he had got up early enough to go with him into the village. He liked to be seen with his father, and it didn't happen very often. He thought about running after him, but his mother thrust a bowl of mashed banana into his hands and told him to eat before he did anything else. He plonked himself down at the table, which rocked unsteadily on its fragile wooden legs.

'We could mend this while we're at it,' he said, rocking the table deliberately to show his mother how precarious it was.

'There are more important things at the moment, so leave it alone,' said Mrs Camara. 'And give it a good wipe when you've finished.'

She lobbed a damp cloth in his direction. Pascal caught it, saw Angeline come through the door, shouted 'Catch!' and threw it at her. He missed badly and knocked a large bowl of bulgar wheat on to the floor. The bowl broke and the wheat rolled everywhere.

'Oh, Pascal!' his mother cried. 'Look what you've done. How can you be so clumsy?' She dropped to her knees and began to scrape the wheat into her hands. Angeline shot him a fierce look, then joined her mother on the floor.

'Sorry, Maman,' Pascal muttered. 'It was an accident. I was only having a bit of fun.'

Bijou started to cry. Pascal picked her up and carried her outside, blowing raspberries on her cheeks and allowing her to bend his fingers backwards.

'It wasn't my fault, was it?' he said to her. 'Maman threw the cloth first.'

He walked to the path and looked down the road, wishing once again that he could have gone with his father. It would have been the perfect time to ask him all the questions he wanted answered, and he would have avoided upsetting his mother. He hoped that his father would stay home long enough to cheer his mother up.

Olivier appeared round the corner, carrying a sling-shot. 'We're all going hunting in the woods,' he said. 'Do you want to come?'

Pascal shook his head. 'Papa's come home. I'm helping him.'

Olivier looked at him quizzically. 'Babysitting?'

Pascal put Bijou on the ground. 'Course not. We're going to mend the fence.'

Olivier pulled a face. 'Suit yourself,' he said. 'I know what I'd rather do.'

'I don't see Papa very much,' Pascal replied.

Olivier pulled another face. 'We might not be able to go hunting for much longer,' he said, marching off.

Pascal took Bijou indoors to Angeline, who set about braiding her hair.

His mother pointed to the bowl of banana. 'You haven't eaten your breakfast,' she said accusingly.

Pascal sat down in front of the browning mess and picked at it slowly. 'Why did Olivier say we might not be able to go hunting for much longer?' he asked.

'Who knows why your cousins say the things they do,' Mrs Camara replied. 'Anyway, I thought you didn't care for hunting.'

It was true. He didn't. He felt sorry for the birds and small animals that they felled with their slingshots.

He had once picked up a wounded firefinch, its leg broken, its rump bloody. The bird had nestled on its side in his hand, its head leaning against his fingers, heart beating fast, until its eyes gradually closed and its body lay still. Pascal had wanted to cry. He had killed other birds and animals before, but had never picked one up, never watched one die right before his very eyes. He had refused to go hunting for days after that, only resuming because he didn't want his cousins to start calling him names.

'Did you hear the gunfire in the night again?' he asked.

His mother looked at him and sighed – in exasperation, he thought – then sat down beside him. 'It's not your job to worry,' she said. 'Leave that to your father and me.'

'But nobody tells me anything,' Pascal complained. 'I'm not a baby any more.'

'There's nothing to tell,' said Mrs Camara. 'There's unrest in some of the towns and a few rebels are causing problems further south, but it's nothing that affects us.'

'What if it gets worse?' Pascal wanted to know.

'I'm sure the government won't let it, and what happens in towns is completely different from what happens in our villages. Nobody is interested in us.'

Once again Pascal had the feeling that he was being protected from the truth, but when his mother sent him to fetch water he knew the conversation was closed. He was delighted, therefore, to see his father returning with a cart full of bamboo.

'Hey, Papa,' he called. 'Maman says I can help you mend the fence.'

'Did she now?' Mr Camara replied. 'Then you can start by fetching me a big cup of water.'

Pascal ran in to pour some water from the bucket. 'What next?' he asked his father as he passed him the cup.

Mr Camara drank the water thirstily. 'Next you can find a knife to cut the raffia.'

Pascal ran indoors again.

'Make sure you don't blunt it,' warned his mother.

He took the knife to his father. 'Will you show me how to weave the raffia?' he asked.

'You can watch and learn,' Mr Camara replied.

They walked over to the bamboo fence that screened their two huts from the path. Sections of it had broken away, leaving gaps and making the whole structure vulnerable.

'It won't protect us, will it?' said Pascal.

'Protect us from what?' asked his father.

'From rebels or refugees.'

Mr Camara looked at him searchingly. 'What do you know about things like that?'

'Nothing much, except I can hear the gunfire and Olivier says we're surrounded by rebels.'

Pascal expected his father to deny there was anything wrong, just as his mother and sister had done. Instead, Mr Camara sat down with him on a rock and explained that insurgents from Sierra Leone and Liberia were causing problems along the border and that a few Guinean rebels had joined them. But government forces were trying to calm it all down, and law and order would be re-established soon.

'Has anyone been killed?' Pascal asked.

'A number of rebels and soldiers,' his father replied dismissively.

Pascal thought about that. 'They're still people,' he said.

'Rebels get what they ask for,' said his father. 'And soldiers – it's their job. Now, are we going to get this fence done?'

The question Pascal really wanted to ask was whether his father thought the rebels would come to their village. In the end he didn't need to ask. When they had finished repairing the fence, his father picked up the planks of wood he had brought home the day before and built two barricades to go across the doors of their huts.

Chapter 7

The heap of cocoa pods was waiting for them at the edge of a field. The pods shone golden and scarlet in the thin early morning sunlight. A small lizard scuttled backwards and forwards over them, perplexed perhaps by the sudden mountainous terrain. Pascal poked at it with a stick, then blocked its path with his machete in whichever direction it tried to go.

'Look at it,' said Kojo. 'It's going mental.'

The lizard disappeared finally underneath one of the pods and didn't reappear.

'That lizard's not stupid, eh?' Tiene chuckled. 'It knows you might chop its head off if it stays around too long.'

Pascal sank his machete into the hard shell of a pod once and then a second time. The pod split open, revealing the stack of cream-coloured beans cocooned inside. He scooped them out in one go and dropped them on to a mat.

'I hate this job the most,' said Kojo. 'I always get shouted at because I can't open the pods neatly like you do.'

'That's because you've got skinny little arms with muscles the size of those beans,' grinned Pascal.

'That big?' laughed Tiene. Though he was only nine months older than Kojo, he was taller, broader and much more skilful at breaking open the pods. 'I'd rather do this than carry sacks all day long. My back's still killing me from the last time.' He broke into a pod and emptied the beans on to the pile.

Kojo saw Mr Kouassi approaching. He quickly placed a pod on the ground in front of him and hit it with his machete. He caught the side and the pod rolled away, its surface barely scratched. He attacked it again, but in his anxiety he missed once more. The overseer was striding towards him as he took aim for a third time. Instead of removing a neat slice, he broke the pod in two, smashing some of the beans on the way. Le Cochon was now hovering over him.

'How many pods can a good breaker open and empty in an hour?' asked the overseer.

'Five hundred, sir,' said Kojo.

'Are you a good breaker?' Le Cochon continued.

Kojo bit his lip and didn't answer.

'Are you a good breaker?' the overseer insisted.

'He's doing his best,' Pascal intervened.

'Then his best ain't good enough,' Le Cochon snapped. 'And who asked for you to join in?'

Pascal glared at him. 'He's only young,' he said. 'You can't expect him to do as well as a grown man.'

'I can expect him to do more than he does. I can expect him to have learnt how to break open a pod without smashin' the beans to pieces.'

'I'm getting better, sir. When I'm stronger I'll be quicker,' Kojo pleaded.

'Perhaps we can't wait that long,' said Le Cochon. 'Perhaps we should get rid of you now instead of wastin' our money on you.'

'Please, Mr Kouassi, please don't do that. I need my wages for my family. I promise I'll try harder.' Kojo was desperate now. 'I'll do anything you say, anything, but please don't send me away.'

'*Please don't send me away*,' Le Cochon imitated. 'And there was me thinkin' you might prefer to be somewhere else.'

'We'd all prefer to be somewhere else,' Pascal growled.

'But that's the trouble, ain't it?' said Le Cochon. 'There ain't nowhere else for you to go in the whole wide world. We're doin' you a favour givin' you a place 'ere, and it ain't no kindergarten, so get on with your work now.' He swung his stick in the air menacingly, laughed when Kojo cowered, then sauntered away whistling loudly.

'Fat pig,' Pascal hissed. 'If I had my gun he'd be dead.'

For the second time that morning, his frustration at having to put up with anything the overseer dealt them threatened to overwhelm him. He was in danger of losing control, and if he did, he would make life more difficult for all the other boys as well as himself. He had to wait until the time was right, however long that might be.

'I should have told him I wanted to leave,' said Kojo. 'I should have told him to stick his job and that I didn't care if he throws me out.'

'So why didn't you?' asked Pascal.

'You know why,' Kojo snapped.

Tiene started humming and broke into another cocoa pod. 'These beans,' he said, holding up a handful, 'they mean money. These beans get turned into chocolate and people all over the world pay money for chocolate. Lots of money. And money means freedom. The trouble is, they don't give us any of the money. No money, no freedom.'

'One day I'll have enough money,' said Kojo, throwing a stone across the ground.

'Then you'd better get those muscle beans working, or they'll dock your pay again,' scoffed Pascal.

Chapter 8

Mr Camara continued to stay at home. Pascal's parents could no longer hide the fact that they were concerned about the news of rebel activity in nearby towns. His father regularly walked to the centre of the village to meet with the village elders. They gathered in Mr Bon's bicycle repair shop to listen to the radio and, very occasionally, to watch news broadcasts on a borrowed television. Wired up to an old car battery, the radio crackled away about unrest on several borders, raids by disaffected mercenaries and clampdowns by government forces. Pascal was forbidden from going into the shop, but his cousins, who hid round the back and listened through a grille in the wall, reported what they heard – with great relish.

None of them was allowed to go off into the forest any more. If they wanted to play shoot-'em-up games, they had to confine themselves to the immediate neighbourhood of the village. Pascal was relieved. He didn't feel safe going too far from home and it didn't seem right to play with pretend guns when people were being killed by real guns.

He was overjoyed when his father finally sat down with him to teach him a card game, but Mr Camara became impatient with him when he kept forgetting the rules and he quickly found something else to do. Once again, Pascal felt that he had failed to live up to his father's expectations.

'I think Papa thinks I'm stupid,' he said to his mother when his father was out.

'Of course he doesn't!' Mrs Camara sounded shocked. 'Why do you say that?'

Pascal shrugged his shoulders. 'He gets annoyed with me if I can't do things.'

'Your father's got a lot on his mind, that's all. He's very proud of you.'

'I'm not good at anything,' Pascal replied.

'You're good at plenty of things and you're good at being you. You're unique and you're blessed,' smiled his mother. 'What more can you ask for? As for your father, he's just no good at showing how he feels.'

Pascal wasn't convinced and became more determined than ever that, one day, his father would want to tell the whole world how proud he was of his son.

I just need to do something, or be something, he thought.

He had no idea what, and was relieved when his cousins called round, inviting him to fish for tiddlers with them in the nearby stream.

'What's your papa like with you?' he asked Bobo on the way over.

'What do you mean?'

'Does he . . . approve of you?'

'Approve?' Bobo pulled a face. 'I've never really thought about it. I guess he does, except when I don't do what he tells me to do. Then he puts on his big, deep voice and roars at me like an angry lion. He's always roaring at Kamil because Kamil never does as he's told.'

'My papa thinks Kamil will go far,' mumbled Pascal.

'Our papa thinks he's a pain in the butt, and so do I most of the time.'

'I think Papa thinks I'm a bit . . . soft, or something.'

Bobo nodded his head, much to Pascal's dismay, then said, 'You're not soft, but you're sort of quiet and a bit thoughtful. Nothing wrong with that. We can't all be the same.'

Pascal wanted to argue, wanted to defend himself, but he didn't. They walked on in silence until they reached the stream, where several of the village women were washing clothes, and where Kamil and Olivier were already splashing their way towards a small waterfall. In a moment of abandon, Pascal threw himself in and raced after them, legs pumping, arms rotating like a whirling dervish. When he caught them up, he pushed Kamil over and stood above him, laughing hysterically.

Kamil hauled himself up. 'What did you do that for, jerk?' he growled. He jabbed Pascal in the chest.

'It was only a bit of fun,' Pascal said, still laughing. He looked for support from Bobo and Olivier. They avoided his gaze.

'I don't call that fun,' Kamil hissed. 'What's got into you?' He bent down and looked at his knee, which was livid with blood.

Pascal stopped laughing and bit his lip. 'Sorry, Kamil,' he said. 'I didn't mean to hurt you.'

'*Sorry, Kamil*,' Kamil imitated. 'You didn't hurt me all right, but you're lucky I'm not going to punch you.'

'Let's forget it, eh?' said Bobo. 'Let's go get those tiddlers.'

Pascal wanted to go home, but he knew it would make things worse. He didn't know where the impulse to lark around and push Kamil over had come from, but it made him look like a fool, and now he wished he could disappear. Along with the others, he waved his net in the water, but had no interest in how many fish fell into it, or what type they were, or whether they were big enough to eat. Kamil teased him regularly about his inability to catch or kill anything with scales or wings, making him feel smaller and more insignificant than ever.

He was glad when, as the shadows lengthened and the village women gathered in their washing, it was time for them to return home to help with chores and sit down for their evening meal. They heard gunfire as they returned along the path. It was too far away to cause them undue concern, but Pascal found himself walking faster, only to slow down again when he realised that he was leaving the others behind.

As soon as he was in sight of his homestead, he sprinted over to where Bijou was watching Angeline grind manioc. He picked her up and swung her backwards and forwards through his legs.

'Mind you don't make her sick,' Angeline smiled. 'She's only just finished eating.'

Pascal lifted Bijou on to his shoulders and galloped round the yard. 'She's all right, aren't you, mon petit chou-fleur?' he called up to her. Bijou giggled and squealed loudly. Pascal put her down again. 'Time to collect eggs,' he said.

'Egg,' Bijou repeated after him.

He put her in the tin bath and pulled her across the grass from one of the chickens' favourite laying places to another. Every time Pascal plucked an egg from its hiding place and gave it to Bijou, she shrieked, 'egg, egg', and cradled it gently in her lap. When they had collected four eggs, and Bijou was in danger of letting them roll into the bottom of the bath, Pascal fashioned a nest of straw for her to put them in, then began to pull her carefully back towards Angeline.

'You're good with her,' Angeline said, nodding approvingly. 'Plenty of boys can't be bothered with babies.'

'She's funny,' said Pascal. He picked Bijou up and rubbed noses with her. Bijou giggled loudly and grabbed his hair. 'She's funny, when she's not pulling my hair,' he yelped.

Pascal blew raspberries on her tummy until she let go, then turned to see his father coming up the path. Mr Camara's face was set and he scarcely acknowledged them as he crossed the yard and went indoors.

'Something's up,' said Angeline. She put down the pestle she had been using to grind the manioc.

'Do you think it's bad news?'

'It certainly doesn't look like good news,' his sister replied, tipping the prepared manioc into a bowl. 'We'd better go and find out. I'll get the eggs.'

Chapter 9

The midday sun beat down on their backs. Heaps of empty pods lay scattered about – temporary shelters for the myriad insects that toiled through the grass. The cocoa beans sweated on their mats, every last trace of moisture destined to be sucked out of them over the following days.

Kojo was humming and occasionally breaking into song.

'D'you hear that, Tiene?' Pascal called. 'It's the mating call of the greater spotted hairy baboon.'

'That's a Salif Keita song I'm singing,' Kojo retorted. 'He's the best.'

'*He* might be,' said Pascal, 'but you're not. Didn't your maman ever tell you that you can't sing?'

'She thought I had a nice voice. You're just jealous.' Kojo began to sing even more loudly.

Pascal brought his machete down on to the head of

a pod with a vicious smack. The pod shattered, spilling some of its beans on the ground. Pascal stamped on them until they were flattened.

'Don't do that!' Kojo protested. 'You'll have Le Cochon after us again.'

Pascal shrugged his shoulders. 'Right now, he'll have his face in a trough and then he'll be snoring in his hammock.'

Tiene rushed around, snorting like a pig. When he dropped on all fours and snuffled about amongst the trampled beans, Kojo joined in, giggling uncontrollably, and tried to barge Tiene over. He wasn't strong enough. Tiene knocked him over instead and stuffed a handful of beans down the front of his shorts.

'Ha!' Pascal laughed. 'More muscles for you.'

Kojo struggled to his feet, the beans dropping out through the bottom of his shorts.

'Yuck!' screeched Tiene. 'Look what he did, look what he did!'

Kojo was about to throw his own handful of beans when one of the other boys warned that someone was coming. In unison, they each picked up a pod, raised their machetes and buried them into the shells once, then again.

As Pascal emptied the contents of a pod, he looked

round to see a small boy approaching, his back bent double under the weight of the sack he was carrying, his face taut from the effort of staying upright. Pascal ran over to him and grabbed the sack from his back.

'You shouldn't be doing that,' he said angrily. He dropped the sack on to the pile of untouched pods.

The boy stood in front of him, eyes red from exhaustion and wide with fear.

'You're frightening him,' said Kojo. 'It's not his fault.'

'I know it's not his fault,' snapped Pascal. 'Do I look stupid all of a sudden? How old are you, boy, and what's your name?'

The boy looked anxious to get away, but Pascal took his arm gently and asked him again.

'Name: Didier. Age: nine. I go now.'

'Didier!' squealed Kojo. 'His name's Didier!'

Pascal gave him a withering look.

'Drogba! Drogba! Drogba!' Tiene chanted. 'He's gonna wipe the smile off the faces of all those other countries. Vive Didier Drogba! Vives Les Éléphants! We're gonna crush those other teams.' He placed a cocoa pod in front of his feet, took four long steps backwards, then ran towards it. He made to kick it with all his might, but right at the last moment lifted his foot over the top.

'Goal!' he cried. He pulled his T-shirt over his head and skipped around, punching the air with his fists. When he stopped and pulled his T-shirt down, he saw that Pascal was glaring at him, while Kojo had resumed his work. He sniffed loudly and turned his back on Pascal. 'Just cos you're not from here,' he muttered.

'I don't want to be from here,' Pascal retorted. 'You can keep your stinking country and your stinking football team.' He turned back to the boy, who was trying to get away. 'Where have you come from, Didier?' he asked. 'We won't hurt you, don't be scared.'

'Far, very far,' muttered Didier. 'Go now or big trouble.' He started to run.

Pascal let him go, but hurled his machete across the ground in anger. 'What are they doing bringing kids that young in here?' he growled.

Kojo and Tiene didn't answer.

'It'll kill him,' Pascal continued. 'He only looks about six.'

'You had it worse,' Kojo said quietly.

'What would you know?' said Pascal. 'Anyway, I'm tough. I've always been tough. That kid won't be able to hack it.'

'What do you care all of a sudden?' Kojo asked. 'It's the same for all of us.'

'Someone has to.'

'You never did before.'

It was true, Pascal had to admit to himself. But there was something about the young boy's face that reminded him of himself when he was that age. He hadn't always been tough, whatever he might have said to Kojo.

'Maybe I've had enough,' Pascal sighed. He picked up the sack of pods and tipped them on to the pile, just as another boy arrived with a sack.

'Better not let Le Cochon see you slacking,' the boy said. 'He's already on the warpath.'

'Ha! He's always on the warpath,' said Tiene. 'What's Mr Piggy upset about this time, Youssouf?'

'Herve dropped a cocoa pod on his trotter and he thinks Herve did it on purpose.'

'Did he?' Kojo asked.

'Would you?' Youssouf sniggered.

'So Le Cochon's footballing days are over,' Tiene said, laughing.

'Before they've even begun,' Kojo sniffed.

'Perhaps we could arrange to drop one on the other trotter as well,' Pascal joined in. 'Or on his head.'

Tiene pretended to thump his head with a pod. 'Ow, ow, ow!' he shrieked. 'My head feels like it's gonna burst.' He dropped to the ground, waggled his legs in the air, then fell still.

'Whoops! The Pig has snuffed it.' Youssouf grinned. 'Better bury him.' He began to heap discarded pods on top of Tiene, but a warning shout made him empty his sack and run off through the bushes.

Pascal saw Mr Kouassi marching towards them, his stained shirt stretched tight over his enormous belly. He was wielding a bicycle chain in his right hand and a stick in his left.

'Stay where you are and do as I say,' Pascal hissed at Tiene. He knelt on the floor beside him and cupped Tiene's head in his hands. 'Close your eyes and pretend you've fainted.'

'What the hell's goin' on?' the overseer yelled.

'It's Tiene,' said Pascal. 'He needs water. The sun's got to him.'

'*I'll* get to him if he don't go back to work. If he can't do the job, he can get out and we'll find somebody else to do it. On your feet, slacker.'

'Really, Mr Kouassi, he's not at all well. He could die if he doesn't have some water soon.'

Pascal could sense the overseer hesitating. He wouldn't want a death on his hands. Tiene groaned theatrically – too theatrically, Pascal thought, and when he felt Le Cochon breathing heavily right behind him, his shoulders tensed. He waited for the stick to land on his back.

'He don't look that bad to me,' Le Cochon said finally. Then he demanded of Kojo, 'You, fetch some water and be quick about it. You others, get on with your work or you'll soon know what it feels like to be ill.' He hauled Pascal up by the back of his T-shirt. 'You too,' he ordered. 'He don't need you fussin' over him like some big soft mama.'

Pascal turned on him, fists clenched, and stared him in the eyes.

'Go on,' Le Cochon goaded him. 'I dare you.'

'I wouldn't waste my energy,' Pascal growled.

The overseer pulled away, then lashed the ground with the bicycle chain right by Pascal's feet. 'You're livin' on borrowed time,' he spat. 'You don't seem to understand who's in charge 'ere and what that means.'

'I understand,' said Pascal.

'Then get your butt over to the plantation before I redesign your legs with this.' He stretched the bicycle chain out in front of Pascal's face. 'Don't push me, son, d'you hear? Just don't push me.'

Chapter 10

Pascal's father was told that he had to return to work.

'It doesn't matter how much I argue that I need to be here to protect my family, they still insist that I go back,' he raged. 'And if I don't, I won't have a job to go back to.'

Pascal, his mother and Angeline were sitting at the table, discussing Mr Camara's news over their supper. Pascal was astonished that his father's job was in danger. He had always believed that it was his father who made the decisions about who did what at the mines. He had never really thought that he could be answerable to somebody else. It had certainly never occurred to him that somebody could take his father's job away from him just like that.

'Don't they understand that the situation here is worrying?' his mother asked.

'The situation is contained, as far as they're aware. From what they read and hear, there's little chance of the fighting escalating beyond the border areas. They have work that needs to be done,' Mr Camara replied, 'and I am the one to do it. If I'm not there it doesn't get done, with the result that they'll have to find someone else.'

'They're putting the greed for diamonds in front of the safety of our family,' said Angeline.

'And we've never even seen a diamond,' added Pascal.

Their mother sighed deeply. 'If your father has to go back, he has to go back, and that's all there is to it. I'm sure we'll be fine, and we can't afford for him to lose his job.'

There was little else to add. They spent the rest of the meal in silence, each pondering what Mr Camara's absence would mean for them. Pascal watched his father light up a cigarette and go outside. He wished he could think of something interesting to say to him, something that would make him realise that his son was worthy of his respect, something he would remember when he was far away from his family with only his work colleagues for company.

What would Kamil say? he wondered. Then he decided that he didn't care, because he wasn't Kamil, he never would be Kamil, so it was pointless to try and think like Kamil.

He wandered to the door. His father had his back to him, a plume of smoke rising above his head.

Pascal hesitated before saying, 'Will you be back for my birthday, Papa?'

His father turned towards him. 'Hmm?'

'I'll be eleven in two weeks' time. Will you be able to come home again?'

'I'm sorry, son, but I don't think I'll be able to have more time away.' Mr Camara took a deep drag of his cigarette and watched for Pascal's reaction.

'That's all right,' Pascal replied, hiding his disappointment. 'I understand. You must be important for them to want you there so badly. I'm glad my papa is important.'

His father nodded. 'We'll celebrate your birthday when I come back,' he said.

'I'll look after Maman and my sisters while you're away.'

Mr Camara grinned. 'Why so grown up all of a sudden?'

'Because I need to be,' replied Pascal. 'Because the situation here is worrying.'

His father grinned again. 'Your mother's a little over-anxious,' he said. 'Don't believe everything you hear. The government is in control.'

'What time are you leaving?' Pascal asked.

'Midday tomorrow.'

'I'm glad it's not a schoolday, so I can say goodbye properly.' Pascal watched for his father's reaction.

'What's so different this time?' Mr Camara said casually. 'I'll be back soon enough.'

'I miss you, that's all,' said Pascal.

'You'll be all right.' His father stubbed out his cigarette, touched Pascal briefly on the shoulder and went back inside.

Chapter 11

It was a grey and humid morning. Pascal remembered it well later on, that ominous backdrop. It was as if the sky were pressing down, refusing to allow any fresh air or light to pass through, in an attempt to suffocate all living things. Mr Camara was tetchy. He was always tetchy when it was time for him to return to work. Pascal wasn't sure whether it was because he wanted to stay, or because he was anxious to be on his way.

Bijou had developed a nasty rash that had become infected, so Mrs Camara left early to take her to the fortnightly clinic in the village, promising to be back before it was time for her husband to catch his bus.

'What if there's a long queue at the clinic?' he protested.

'Then I'll ask if I can move forward,' replied Mrs Camara. 'I'm sure people will understand.'

'Well, I can't wait if you're not back,' he said. 'The bus won't wait for me.'

'Of course not,' said Mrs Camara. 'And I will be back to say goodbye.'

Pascal wondered if his father thought Bijou shouldn't go to the clinic, he was making such a fuss about it. Angeline attempted to calm him down by putting a large bowl of freshly sliced fruit in front of him. He picked at it half-heartedly, then pushed it away and went outside to have a cigarette. While he was there, he walked by the fence, checking that nothing had shifted since he had repaired it. Pascal watched him from the doorway, until Angeline asked him to fetch some more water so that she could wash the dishes. He grabbed the bucket and ran off down the path. Even if his father wasn't being very friendly, he didn't want to miss these last few moments with him. It might be some time before he came home again.

Pascal spotted Kamil and Olivier ahead of him, walking towards the pump. At first, he wanted to turn back and wait until they had gone. Then he thought about overtaking them, but decided he'd better not. Instead, he caught up with them and walked alongside.

'You all right?' Kamil asked.

'Why?'

'Your papa goes back today, doesn't he?'

Pascal nodded.

'Do you wanna play football with us this afternoon?' said Olivier.

Pascal nodded again, though he wasn't sure. He didn't really feel like doing anything.

'Mr Bon says he'll have the television in his shop later, so we can watch the big match,' said Olivier. 'Vive Le Syli Nationale!'

Pascal had forgotten all about it. The Guinean team was due to play a friendly against Nigeria. All the village men and boys gathered at the bicycle repair shop whenever there was a match to be watched. If only his father didn't have to go back. It had been a long time since they had watched a football game together.

'Vive Le Syli Nationale,' he echoed, trying to sound enthusiastic.

They reached the water pump. Kamil filled his two jugs, put one on the ground, then, without warning, swung the other towards Pascal. A stream of water flew from the jug and soaked the front of Pascal's shorts. The water was so cold that Pascal froze with shock while Kamil hooted with laughter.

'Too slow, too slow!' he chanted. 'He-he, you wet yourself, little bro.'

A barrage of gunfire stripped the smile from his face.

'Shit! That was really close!' Olivier shrieked.

A second barrage was followed by a devastating explosion.

'Run!' Pascal yelled.

They hurtled down the path towards the village. Another explosion stopped them for an instant while they worked out where the sound had come from. There was shouting now from all around – and more gunfire.

'Keep going!' Olivier yelled.

When their homesteads came into view, Pascal felt a surge of relief. Mr Camara was framed in the doorway.

'Papa!' he cried out. 'What's happen—'

A burst of gunfire obliterated the rest of his words. His father shouted something that he didn't hear. There was a blinding flash of light. An enormous explosion almost blew Pascal off his feet. Then all he could see was flames. Flames licking at the bamboo fence. Flames lapping at the brittle grass. Another explosion. His father's face. Screams. Gunfire. Thudding feet. Shiny metal. A hand pulling at his arm.

'Come on, Pascal. They're going to kill us,' shouted Olivier.

'Papa!' Pascal screamed.

'It's too late. Let's get out of here.'

Something bit hard into his shoulder. He touched the place with his fingers. It was wet. He pulled his fingers away and looked at them. They were red.

He ran, then, faster than he had ever run in his life. He ran until his lungs threatened to rupture and his legs to collapse, and still he ran. He ploughed along the dusty trail thrown up by Olivier and Kamil before him, until they crashed through the barricade of trees that stood sentry for the length of the forest. Once inside, they swerved this way and that to avoid roots and low plants that hindered their progress as if on purpose. Deeper and deeper they went. Soon, all Pascal could hear were the sounds of his gasps for air and the tripping of his feet. Sweat poured down his face and stung his eyes. He lost sight momentarily of his cousins as the darkness of the inner forest enveloped them.

And then he had to stop. His body refused to obey any more exhortations to keep going and his legs crumpled underneath him. He lay on the ground, prepared just to lie there and accept whatever consequences came his way, before struggling to his feet again to search for Kamil and Olivier.

He found them close by, sprawled over a pile of logs. Kamil was retching and crying. Olivier, like Pascal, was trying to catch his breath. They could hear sporadic gunfire in the distance, but at that moment the forest cradled them in its arms.

None of them spoke. Kamil began to rock backwards and forwards, while his crying turned into a low moan. Olivier sat with his head buried in his hands. Pascal squatted on the forest floor, his back against a tree, unable to think beyond the notion that they were still in danger, unable to see beyond the bright white light that flashed over and over again in front of his eyes.

Another explosion made him jump to his feet.

'I'm going back,' he said. 'Papa and Angeline need me.'

'You can't go back!' Olivier cried. 'They'll kill you.'

'Papa needs me,' Pascal insisted. 'I'm going.'

Olivier leapt to his feet and grabbed hold of him. 'Your papa doesn't need you,' he said firmly. 'You know he doesn't. But we do. If we stick together we'll be safer.'

'And Maman? She went into the village with Bijou.'

'The only way we can help our families is to stay alive until . . . until the trouble passes.'

Olivier kept his hold on Pascal. Pascal tried to pull away, but gave in when the realisation finally dawned on him that there was nothing he could do.

'Papa will be all right,' he said. 'Papa is strong.'

Olivier looked at him quizzically, then nodded. 'We have to be strong,' he said. He gripped Pascal by the shoulder. Pascal yelped and pulled away. 'You're bleeding,' said Olivier, staring at the blood on his hand.

'Something hit me,' whimpered Pascal. Only now had he become aware of the pain.

'Does it hurt?' asked Olivier.

It hurt like mad, but nowhere near as much as the pain in his head. Pascal grimaced. He wanted to go home. He wanted to feel his mother's arms around him, comforting him, telling him there was nothing to worry about.

'The situation is very worrying,' he muttered. 'Very worrying.'

A loud bang startled them. They ducked down by a bush and listened. There was no other sound. Even the animals had been silenced, if they hadn't already run away. They hissed at Kamil to hide. He was still rocking. His face was vacant.

'He's in a bad way,' said Olivier. 'We can't leave him there.'

They crept over to him, keeping low in case there was somebody else in the forest. Olivier linked his arm through Kamil's and signalled for Pascal to do the same.

Together, they pulled him to his feet and dragged him with them back to the bush. He sat like a rag doll, head lolloping on his chest, until Olivier spoke to him.

'Kamil,' Olivier said. 'You're going to be all right, Kamil. We're going to look after you.'

Kamil stared at him, eyes wide, then he saw Pascal. A look of sheer terror crossed his face and he screamed. 'They killed them,' he cried out. 'They killed them, all of them. I saw your papa. They blew him to pieces.'

Chapter 12

It was even more stifling in the middle of the plantation. A canopy of taller trees protected the cacao trees with their precious crop of cocoa pods by providing them with shade, but it also prevented heat from escaping. As the afternoon wore on, the boys were so exhausted they could scarcely lift their machetes to cut down another pod. Those with a greater reach, like Pascal, used a long-handled cutting tool to tackle the pods that grew higher up. The pain they suffered in their shoulders was excruciating, even after months of doing the same work, day in, day out.

They had been allowed a few minutes' break for a drink of water in between their morning and afternoon jobs, and had dropped to the ground like the pods they were cutting as soon as the whistle went for them to stop. Pascal lay on his back, looking up through the multicoloured patchwork of leaves and fruits, the sunlight dipping this way and that and sewing their edges with gold. For a brief moment, he allowed himself to appreciate the beauty of it, before he succumbed to the effort of keeping his eyes open and allowed them to close.

Kojo rolled over to him. 'You're not going to sleep, are you?' he asked.

Pascal grunted.

'I'll warn you if someone comes,' Kojo continued, before humming quietly.

Pascal grunted again.

'That boy doesn't care any more,' said Tiene, who was lying close by and flicking ants with a stick. 'He's waiting to get his head bitten off.'

'I'll bite yours off if you don't shut up,' muttered Pascal.

'Now why would you want to do that, when my head's full of shit,' chuckled Tiene. He flicked a large ant, which landed in Pascal's hair.

Kojo glared at him for trying to annoy Pascal, but watched in fascination as the ant made its way out of the hair, down his friend's forehead and on to his nose. Pascal didn't make any effort to remove it, even when the ant began to investigate the edges of his nostrils. Then, in one swift movement, he leapt to his feet, brushing the ant from his face, and threw himself on top of Tiene, pinning him to the ground.

'Did you do that?' he growled.

'Do what?' Tiene puffed.

'You know what.'

'There are a lot of flying ants around at this time of the year.' Tiene snickered.

'Very funny,' said Pascal. 'Do you know what you are? You're a major pain in the butt because you never shut up.'

'And you never lighten up,' Tiene retorted fiercely. 'At least I try and have a bit of fun. At least I don't spend all day long being grumpy. You don't even know what fun is.'

Pascal felt an overwhelming sense of outrage and injustice welling up inside. Hadn't he saved this boy from a beating earlier that day? Hadn't he had to face things in his life that Tiene could never begin to understand? How dare he lie there and judge him. His hands tightened in anger and he began to shake uncontrollably. He'd had enough of people pushing him around, accusing him, persecuting him.

'Stop, Pascal, stop! You're hurting him.' Kojo's voice first, and then his fists, pummelling his back, trying to beat him off. 'Leave him, Pascal.'

He pushed at Pascal's shoulder with all his might, until Tiene managed to twist his torso round and partially free himself. Pascal toppled to the side and Tiene crawled out of his reach.

'You were trying to kill me!' Tiene hissed. He rubbed his neck, coughing harshly.

Pascal shuddered and curled up into a tight ball.

Kojo stood between them, looking anxiously from one to the other. 'Pascal?' he said quietly.

'I should report him,' said Tiene. 'He's a lunatic.'

'He's not a lunatic,' said Kojo. 'You don't understand.'

'I understand that he had his hands around my neck.'

'He didn't mean it,' Kojo insisted. 'I'm sure —' He stopped when he saw that Pascal's body was shaking. 'Pascal,' he said again, 'are you all right?'

A low howl of anguish startled both Kojo and Tiene. They looked at each other in astonishment. Pascal was crying. Kojo wanted to bend down to him, to touch his arm just to let him know that he was there for him.

Tiene held him back. 'Don't,' he hissed. 'He might go for you. Nobody wants to be seen crying, especially Pascal. Leave him alone.'

'He's my friend. I can't just leave him alone. What if Le Cochon comes? It must be nearly time to go back to work.'

'It's not my problem,' Tiene said dismissively. 'Why should I care when he just tried to kill me?' He walked away, humming tunelessly and kicking at the leaves that covered the ground.

Kojo stood, wondering what to do. The whistle blew and he knew that Le Cochon or one of the other overseers would be heading in their direction. Pascal was now completely still and silent.

'Pascal,' Kojo called quietly. 'We've got to get back to work.'

There was no response. He hesitated for a few moments longer, then began to move over to where he had dropped his machete. He heard a scuffling noise and turned to see that Pascal was on his feet. He smiled at him, but Pascal seemed not to notice. Kojo walked very slowly, hoping that his friend would catch up with him, but Pascal strode past him without a word, picked up his cutter and resumed his work.

Pascal remained silent for the rest of the day. When Tiene and Youssouf tried to goad him by calling him a nutcase and a lunatic, he ignored them. At one point, Mr Kouassi stood by him and watched him work.

'I'm impressed,' he said. 'If you can cut down that many pods today, why can't you cut down that many pods every day?'

Pascal didn't answer.

'Seems to me that if you can cut down that many pods one day, you must be slackin' on them other days,' the overseer continued. 'Seems like all them other boys must be slackin' too.' He cracked the bicycle chain hard on the ground. 'D'you hear me? Seems like you other boys are slackin', and what happens to slackers?'

The boys tried to speed up as he moved to each of them in turn and stood behind them, breathing heavily while he jangled the bicycle chain and lashed the undergrowth with his stick.

'What happens to slackers?' he repeated.

'They get beaten,' the boys replied.

'And why do they get beaten?' asked Le Cochon.

'Because slackers waste the boss's money,' said the boys.

'Louder,' ordered Le Cochon.

'Slackers waste the boss's money,' the boys shouted.

Le Cochon was looking directly at Pascal when he barked his last order. Pascal stayed tight-lipped, staring down at his hands, which were holding the cutting tool.

'What's the matter? Have you lost your tongue?' Le Cochon barked. 'I asked what happens to slackers, and you ain't told me.'

Pascal raised his head and stared at him. He didn't say a word.

'You been cryin', boy?'

Pascal didn't answer.

'I'll make you cry for your insolence,' Le Cochon snarled. He raised the bicycle chain and brought it down on Pascal's back.

Pascal winced with pain, but didn't utter a word.

'You want some more, do you?' Le Cochon demanded.

'Don't, sir, please don't,' Kojo cried.

The overseer ignored him, swinging the chain and catching Pascal round the back of his legs. Pascal fell to the ground, biting his lip to prevent himself from screaming.

'Please don't hit him again,' Kojo begged.

'Leave him, sir,' Tiene joined in. 'He's hurt enough.'

Le Cochon swung round as though he were about to hit Tiene as well, but instead he growled at them to get back to work and lumbered off.

Kojo and Tiene helped Pascal to his feet. His legs were bleeding and covered in livid welts, and blood was seeping through his T-shirt.

'Are you OK?' asked Kojo.

Pascal nodded his head, though when he tried to walk his legs collapsed. Kojo and Tiene helped him to a tree stump.

'We should do something about that pig,' said Tiene. 'He shouldn't be allowed to get away with that.'

Pascal looked up at him. 'I'm sorry,' he said. 'Sorry for what I did. I just lost it.'

'It happens,' replied Tiene. 'And I know I'm an annoying little rat.' He fell to the ground, squeaking loudly and snuffling through the leaves.

Kojo began to giggle, then Pascal joined in, until all three of them were squeaking and giggling like three-year-olds, stopping only when they were breathless and Youssouf warned them about the noise they were making.

'Better get on with some work before The Pig comes back,' said Pascal.

Chapter 13

'We need to move on,' said Olivier finally. 'We're not safe here. We need to go deeper into the forest.'

Pascal was too shocked to argue. Kamil's outburst had stripped him of any last stubborn deception that what he had seen in front of his very eyes hadn't really taken place. And yet he still tried to believe that it was possible to survive, that his father had survived. He wanted to go back, but was terrified of what he might find. He wanted to know if Angeline was safe. He wanted to search for his mother and Bijou, but was petrified of being caught by the rebels.

'Everyone will have run away,' Olivier insisted. 'Everyone who . . . We'll find them again when it's all over. They'll search for us. They're bound to search for us.'

Pascal was amazed at how calm his cousin seemed to be when he had no idea what had happened to his own family. He was relieved that Olivier was there to make the decisions for him. Olivier had taken charge, kept them together and looked out for them, even though he was less than two years older than Pascal and six months younger than Kamil.

They had heard other voices, other footsteps in the forest. They had thrown themselves to the ground whenever they thought somebody was coming in their direction. In the gloom, with their fears playing havoc with their senses, they couldn't tell who was friend and who was foe. Kamil didn't seem to understand the danger. Sometimes he cried out, sometimes he refused to hide and had to be pulled out of sight. Now, as they went deeper and deeper into the forest, pushing their way past tentacled vines and through tangled undergrowth, Pascal wondered where the boy his father had thought would go far in life had disappeared to. And then, as he thought again of his father, a huge, aching disquiet hit him. He felt nauseous and his head began to swim. He tried to focus on one thing and one thing alone. His mother had not been at home. His mother would find him and everything would be all right.

At last, they felt safe enough to stop for the night. The only sounds they could hear now were made by monkeys high up in the treetops and smaller animals scuttling along the forest floor. They found a narrow piece of ground that was surrounded by low bushes, which screened them when they sat down. Kamil lay on his back and didn't say a word. Olivier stripped the bark off a fallen branch, exploring underneath it to discover what insects were hiding there, as though conducting some sort of field trial. Pascal stood for a while and wandered between one bush and another. He didn't feel safe enough to sit, convinced that if he were still he would be bombarded with unwelcome thoughts.

'You hungry?' Olivier asked suddenly.

Pascal shrugged his shoulders and winced with pain. He felt the place where the bullet had grazed him. It was sticky now, a sign that it had stopped bleeding. The thought of congealed blood made him want to retch, and he was sure he wouldn't be able to eat if someone put food in front of him. 'How long will we have to stay here?' he asked instead.

It was Olivier's turn to shrug his shoulders. 'Tonight. Tomorrow, maybe. Are you scared?'

Pascal wanted to say no, but found himself nodding.

'I am too,' Olivier said simply. 'Flipping scared.'

Pascal sat down next to him. 'We'll be all right, though, won't we?' he asked. 'They won't do anything to kids.' He wanted so much to believe it.

'We won't let them,' replied Olivier. 'We won't let them catch us.'

'What about Kamil?'

'You'll be all right, won't you, Kamil? He'll be all right in the morning,' Olivier said.

Pascal started to cry. He had tried so hard not to, but a surge of terror took hold of him and beat him into submission, leaving him gasping for breath. Olivier moved over to put his arm around him. Pascal sank against him, overwhelmed by exhaustion.

'I'm scared to close my eyes,' he sobbed.

Chapter 14

Pascal cursed the wooden pallet for its refusal to allow him just the smallest of hollows to relieve the throbbing soreness of his back. Lying on either side wasn't an option because it rubbed his swollen lower legs, which weren't protected by his shorts. Lying on his front was virtually impossible, the pallet was so hard. On his back, he could cope as long as he took his weight on one shoulder and didn't move, but the pain was unbearable if he tried to shift to the other shoulder.

His physical pain was nothing compared to the mental torment he was suffering. He replayed the scene with Tiene over and over again, trying to understand what had driven him to attack his friend so viciously. Tiene could be irritating, very irritating, but he was funny and tried hard to keep the other boys' spirits up with his ridiculous antics. He hadn't deserved to be assaulted. Besides, it was important to all of them that they stick together and help each other. Pascal knew that more than anyone else. A rift between any of them would make life harder for everyone.

The thing that terrified him most was the thought that, had Kojo not been there to stop him, he might have carried on, might have seriously hurt Tiene, might have . . . Every time he asked himself the question 'Would I have let go of him?', he could not allow himself to reach an answer. Yet the question kept repeating itself. He tried to push it away, but it was there, nagging at him, demanding, insistent.

He closed his eyes and tried to sleep. He couldn't. The pain in his body prevented it. The hunger that wracked him prevented it. The question prevented it. He listened to the other boys. Some were stone-dead silent. Some were muttering. Some were thrashing around, creaking on their wooden pallets.

Pascal wondered if Kojo was asleep. He wasn't moving. They hadn't talked very much that evening, just the odd word here and there after the boys had returned from their corn-paste supper to find Pascal huddled in his corner. The dormitory had been unusually quiet. There was a tension in the air, no one speaking in case it provoked an unwelcome reaction.

Although they had larked around earlier on in order to forget what had happened, when they lay down in the darkness, the memory of that moment of madness joined forces with the other ghosts that haunted them.

I did that, Pascal thought to himself. *I went too far and broke the rules. Why?*

He jumped to his feet and stood at the window. He held the bars and gritted his teeth.

'I've got to get out of here,' he said under his breath. 'I've got to get out of here.'

He heard one of the boys get up and pee into the bucket that served as their latrine. When the boy went to lie down again, he stubbed his toe. He yelped with pain, swore loudly and cursed his pallet bed. Pascal wanted to hiss at him to be quiet, dreading that the other boys might wake up and disturb his thoughts. They didn't, though, and Pascal breathed a sigh of relief.

A moth that must have settled on the inside walls of the dormitory while it was still light suddenly flew past Pascal and away towards the moon. Pascal watched its silhouette grow smaller and smaller until it disappeared, and as he watched he grew more determined that one day, soon, he would escape. He had very little money because none of them had been paid for weeks − the price of chocolate had gone down, they were told − but somehow he would find a way to go back home to his own country and discover what had happened to his mother and sisters. If his father was no longer there to protect them, then he must take over that role.

Kojo stirred and sat up. 'You all right?' he asked.

Pascal nodded in the darkness. 'I'm sorry,' he said. 'About earlier.'

'I've forgotten about it,' said Kojo.

Pascal didn't argue, though he knew it wasn't true. He dropped down next to Kojo. 'I've got to leave,' he said quietly. 'You coming with me?'

He felt his young friend turn towards him questioningly. 'Leave?' asked Kojo, his voice tight. 'When?'

'Soon,' said Pascal. 'Very soon. I know we said we'd wait until we had enough money, but that could be never.'

'How will we manage without?'

'We'll manage. I've got a bit,' Pascal said determinedly. He didn't want Kojo to undermine the decision he had reached, didn't want him to sow doubt. 'You don't have to come with me.'

Kojo didn't reply straight away, but then he said quietly, 'I'll never forget the day Papa lost his job.

I was larking around in the woods with my brother. I'd just hit him with a papaya and was running away, when I saw my father coming across the rickety bridge with his bicycle. It was too early for him to be there. He tried to pretend there was nothing to worry about, but, Pascal, I could see it in his face. He looked old suddenly. I was only eight, but I could tell that something bad had happened. He never recovered from losing his job, and that's when he became ill.' Pascal heard his friend swallow and sniff before continuing. 'I'm not helping my family by staying, and I'm not staying if you're going.'

Pascal pushed him gently on the shoulder. 'You'd miss me too much, wouldn't you?' he chuckled.

'Like a hole in the head,' muttered Kojo. 'How are we going to escape?'

'I dunno yet,' said Pascal. 'I'll have to work something out.'

They sat in silence for a while. Pascal wondered if he had done the right thing in asking Kojo to go with him. Kojo wasn't as strong as he was, physically or mentally, and might cause problems for him. But for some strange reason, even though at times he longed for his own space, he didn't want to undertake this next journey alone. Besides, he had promised Kojo

Chapter 15

Shouts. Mr Camara smoking his cigarette, repairing the fence. Flames licking at the bamboo edges. Kamil flicking playing cards across the table for Pascal to catch, but he misses every time. Laughter. Bright white lights distorting through cut-diamond faces. Flames licking at pounding feet. Angeline throwing Bijou up in the air, over and over, until Bijou doesn't come down again. Screams. Mrs Camara rocking in a chair, worrying. Mr Camara running away when Pascal tries to speak to him, running away when Pascal tries to speak to him, running away . . . Shouts. Loud, urgent.

'Wake up, Pascal! Quick! There's someone coming.'

Olivier was shaking him. Pascal didn't know where he was. He sat up abruptly and looked around. Kamil was standing close by, staring into the distance.

'We've gotta get out of here – now,' Olivier hissed.

'Come on, Kamil, don't just stand there.' He pulled Pascal to his feet. 'Let's go.' He began to run, beckoning them to follow.

'Come on, Kamil,' Pascal urged.

He tugged at Kamil's hand. A burst of gunfire made them both jump and, to Pascal's relief, Kamil began to run with him, soon overtaking him. There were shouts and more gunfire. Pascal felt himself ducking automatically every time the shots rang out, though he had no idea if they were aimed at him. His legs and lungs were soon protesting. A small part of him wanted to give up and take whatever was coming, anything rather than go through the agony of trying to keep up with Olivier. Even Kamil had fallen behind him again now.

And then Pascal noticed that it had gone quiet. Deadly quiet. Ahead of them, Olivier kept running, but more slowly, and turned every so often to look around. At last, he stopped.

'I think we've lost them,' he puffed. 'I can't hear anything any more.'

'How do you know it was us they were after? How do you know they weren't on our side?' Pascal asked.

'It won't be us they were after,' Olivier replied. 'But we don't want to risk being caught, do we?'

'But what if it was someone coming to find us?'

'Pascal, nobody's looking for us. Not now. Not yet.'

Pascal knew he was right, but he struggled to cope with the thought that they were all alone.

'They're all dead.' Kamil spoke for the first time. 'All of them. Dead.'

'Shut up, Kamil,' Olivier hissed. 'You don't know what you're talking about.'

'Bang, bang, you're dead!' Kamil snorted.

A bullet smacked into a tree in front of them. Two men broke through a distant cover of bushes and headed towards them, shouting at them to stay where they were.

'Run!' Olivier shouted.

Pascal froze for a moment, then began to run for his life. Kamil didn't move. Olivier yelled at him to follow but, as the men drew closer to him, Kamil fell to his knees and started to sob and plead and beg them to spare him. Pascal faltered, but his cousin spurred him on.

'We'll have to leave him. We've got no choice,' Olivier insisted.

Pascal's last view of Kamil was of the two rebels, one on either side of him, lifting him up and half dragging, half carrying him away. Kamil was screaming.

Chapter 16

Several hours passed by. Pascal and Olivier squatted under an overhanging rock, screened by a mesh of brambles and vines. Neither of them spoke. They were too exhausted and distraught. The only sound they could hear was a nearby waterfall. They had plunged into it briefly in an effort to revive themselves. Pascal had wanted to stay there with the water beating mercilessly on his head, emptying it of everything, but Olivier had pulled him away to hide. Now its uninterrupted whoosh and burble was somehow comforting, yet it was a danger to them because it stifled any other noise.

They both must have closed their eyes, for Pascal received no warning from Olivier that anything was wrong. Now something was prodding him in the stomach. He went to push it away and felt something cold and hard. He opened his eyes to find a rifle pressed

92